Printed in the U.S.A.

ISBN 0-7172-8330-5

JIM HENSON'S MUPPETS

IN

The Disaster on Wheels

A Book About Helping Others

By Michaela Muntean • Illustrated by Tom Leigh

GROLIER

It was a perfect afternoon for roller skating in the park.

"Look at this!" Janice said as she did a perfect one-foot spin.

"That's great," said Skeeter. "Now try this," as she did a crossover.

From across the playground, Piggy skated slowly toward them. "Watch out!" she cried. Piggy swerved to avoid running into Skeeter . . .

. . . and banged right into Janice. "Watch where you're going, Piggy!" said Janice.

"Sorry," said Piggy.

"You both okay?" Skeeter asked, helping Piggy to her feet.

"I'm fine," said Janice.

"I think I am, too," said Piggy. She looked embarrassed. "Thank goodness for helmets and knee pads."

"Just keep trying," Skeeter said to Piggy as Skeeter and Janice sped away to race each other to the flagpole.

"Poor Piggy," Skeeter said to Janice. "She just can't seem to get the hang of roller skating."

"I know," said Janice. "But she really is kind of a menace on the playground."

Meanwhile, Piggy slowly inched her way
toward a tree. She leaned against it and
watched the other skaters as they glided,
wheeled, and whirled.

She would have given almost anything to skate as well as Skeeter. Being able to skate like Janice was out of the question. Janice was the best skater on the playground. She could do all the fanciest moves.

Actually, Piggy didn't care if she ever learned any fancy moves. All she wanted was to skate in a straight line without running into something or some*one*.

Piggy kept trying. But after running into Fozzie once, and the flagpole twice, she took off her skates and headed for home.

"I guess I'll never be a roller skater," she said to herself.

Janice saw her go, and all of a sudden, she regretted having been mean to Piggy about her skating.

I'll tell her I'm sorry when I see her tomorrow, Janice thought. But Janice didn't get a chance to tell Piggy she was sorry. Piggy didn't show up at the playground the next day.

When she didn't show up the day after that, Janice decided to find out if Piggy was all right. On her way home, she stopped off at Piggy's house.

"Oh, hi," said Piggy when she saw Janice at the door.

"Are you all right?" Janice asked.

"Sure," said Piggy. "Why?"

"You haven't been to the playground lately. I wanted to make sure you were okay," Janice said. "And I wanted to tell you I was sorry for being mean to you the other day."

"I decided roller skating was baby stuff," said Piggy.

"Gee, I didn't know you felt that way," said Janice, feeling a little hurt. Janice didn't think roller skating was baby stuff at all. She turned to go. "I guess I'll see you around," she said.

When Janice got to the end of the walk, Piggy couldn't stand it. "Wait," she cried. "I didn't mean that, Janice. I haven't been to the playground because I'm such a bad skater. I mean, it's so embarrassing to keep running into things!"

"You're not *that* bad a skater," said Janice.

"Let's face it," Piggy said. "I'm a disaster on wheels."

Janice was quiet for a moment. "You know," she said, "I think all you need is a little help, and I'm just the person to help you."

"What do you mean?" Piggy asked.

"I'll help you learn how to roller skate," said Janice. "If we meet early every morning, we'll have the whole playground to ourselves. What do you say, Piggy?"

"Are you sure you want to help me?" Piggy asked.

"Positive," said Janice.

So early the next morning, Janice met
Piggy at the playground for her first lesson.

"Just follow me," Janice said, and she skated quickly to the other side of the playground.

Piggy was quick, too—quick to fall.

"Janice," Piggy said as she got to her feet, "this isn't very helpful. I know you mean well, but if I could skate like you, I wouldn't have a problem."

"Oh, sorry," Janice said. "You're right. It's just that I've never taught anyone how to do anything before. Let's try it again."

Janice took Piggy's hand, and together they skated slowly across the playground.

"Just take slow, gliding steps, like you're walking," Janice said.

For a few days, Janice thought it was fun to teach Piggy how to skate. But Janice liked to sleep late in the mornings. By the third day, she was tired of getting up so early.

She was all set to tell Piggy the lessons were over. But when she got to the playground that morning, Piggy was already there, practicing the things Janice had taught her the day before. They seemed to be working. "Look, Teacher," she said. "How am I doing?"

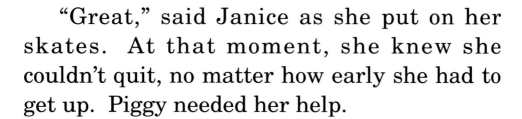

"Great," said Janice as she put on her skates. At that moment, she knew she couldn't quit, no matter how early she had to get up. Piggy needed her help.

So every morning for the next two weeks, Janice helped Piggy learn to roller-skate. She taught her how to skate in a straight line without wobbling. She taught her how to turn, and, most important of all, she taught her how to stop.

With Janice's help, Piggy quickly improved. Soon she had enough confidence to skate by herself.

Janice was proud of her student. "You're doing so well," she said, "that I think it's time for you to face the world."

"You really think so?" asked Piggy.

"You bet I do," said Janice.

So that afternoon, Piggy joined the others on the playground. Janice asked everyone to stop skating for a moment. "I'd like to present my first and finest pupil," she said. Then Piggy glided onto the playground and did a perfect half turn.

"Nice move!" cheered Skeeter as everyone applauded. Piggy felt very proud, and so did Janice.

"I never could have done it without Janice's help," said Piggy. Then she turned to face Janice. "Thanks, Janice," she said.

"You're welcome," Janice replied. "But I have to admit, I didn't do it just for you."

Piggy was puzzled. "Who else could you have done it for?" she asked.

"*Me*," said Janice. "Now instead of bump-
ing into each other, we can roller-skate
together. Besides—it's always more fun for
me when you're around!"

Let's Talk About Helping Others

Sometimes helping another person is easy. But sometimes it takes some work. Janice had to get up early every morning to teach Piggy how to roller-skate. But the good feeling she got from helping was worth all the trouble.

Here are some questions about helping others for you to think about:

You probably have chances to help other people every day. Was there someone you helped today?

How do you feel when you help out? How do you feel when you don't?

There are many different kinds of helping. Can you think of some of them?